The YOUNG DASTAN Chronicles

WALLS of BABYLON

The YOUNG DASTAN Chronicles

WALLS of BABYLON

By Catherine Hapka
Based on characters created for the motion picture
Prince of Persia: The Sands of Time
Based on the Screenplay written by Boaz Yakin and Doug Miro & Carlo Bernard
Screen Story by Jordan Mechner
Based on the videogame series "Prince Of Persia" created by Jordan Mechner
Executive Producers Mike Stenson, Chad Oman, John August,
Jordan Mechner, Patrick McCormick, Eric McLeod
Produced by Jerry Bruckheimer
Directed by Mike Newell

DISNEP PRESS
New York

Copyright © 2010 Disney Enterprises, Inc.
JERRY BRUCKHEIMER FILMS™ and JERRY BRUCKHEIMER FILMS Tree Logo™ are all trademarks. All rights reserved. Unauthorized use is prohibited.

Printed in the United States of America

First Edition
1 3 5 7 9 10 8 6 4 2
J689-1817-1-10182
Library of Congress Catalog Card Number on file.
ISBN 978-1-4231-1006-4
Visit www.disneybooks.com

LONG AGO, in the ancient and sand swept land of Persia, there was a prince whose strength, bravery, and honesty were revered across the land. His name struck fear in his enemies and courage in his men.

This was Dastan.

But before he was to become this prince of legend, Dastan had to survive on the streets of Nasaf, heart of the Persian Empire. It was a place of royal palaces, bustling markets, exotic spices, and beautiful people. But beneath its sleek surface was a rotten underbelly where street kids fought for meager scraps of food and few rules applied.

It is on these streets that the tale of Prince Dastan truly begins. . . .

CHAPTER ONE

"Oof!"

The breath left Dastan's body as the other boy barreled straight into him. They both fell to the ground, Dastan's elbow scraping the dusty street.

The ground was hard in the Persian city of Nasaf. Life was hard, too. At least for someone like Dastan with no home or family.

He felt something squish under his leg. Instantly, the odor of rotten fruit surrounded him.

Dastan ignored the stink. After all, it was

hardly the only unpleasant smell in Nasaf's enormous trash dump. And at the moment, he had bigger concerns.

Scooting both bare feet under him, Dastan flipped himself into a standing position in one fluid movement. His opponent, a stocky thirteen-year-old named Hutan, was up nearly as fast.

"Get him, Dastan!" a voice shouted.

Brushing his brown hair away from his eyes, Dastan glanced over and saw two young brothers among the crowd. The older one was named Yusef as he recalled; Dastan wasn't sure of the younger one's name.

"Don't worry," Dastan called to them, sounding confident. "I'll make certain your bets weren't in vain."

"Don't be so sure," Hutan growled.

He lunged forward. Smoothly, Dastan sidestepped and tripped him. The other boy went sprawling face-first into a pile of spoiled cheese and rice. Dastan's supporters cheered while Hutan's groaned.

Dastan knew he had to act fast. He leaped onto his opponent's back, pressing Hutan's shoulders to the ground and grabbing for his arm. If he could get it pinned behind Hutan's back, this wrestling match would be over. Hutan grunted with annoyance, keeping his arm just out of reach.

"On your feet, boy!" someone shouted at Hutan. "I have a whole handful of figs riding on this fight!"

Dastan didn't care much about the bets the other street rats had made. He cared only for the real prize: a tasty shank of roasted lamb. It was a little burnt, which was probably why someone had tossed it away. But Dastan wasn't picky. He couldn't afford to be. No one out on the streets could be—ever.

Glancing over, he spared the piece of lamb a glance, licking his lips. He'd eaten nothing but a stale crust of bread since yesterday. That meat would fill his hungry belly.

The problem was, he and Hutan had spotted it at the same moment. They'd decided to settle the morsel's ownership in the usual way of the streets: a fight.

"Aaaaaaah!" Hutan howled, flinging himself upward. Dastan tried to hold on, but thoughts of eating had distracted him and Hutan was strong. Dastan went flying off to one side.

By the time he jumped back to his feet, Hutan was coming at him. Dastan braced himself, meeting the larger boy's assault. Using the force of Hutan's move against him, he flipped the other boy over one slim shoulder.

SLAM! Hutan hit the ground with a grunt. The crowd let out a collective "Oooooh!"

Dastan didn't smile often. But now his lips

curled up as he watched Hutan climb to his feet with a groan. He was starting to enjoy himself.

"You rat!" Hutan cried when he'd recovered his breath. He glared at Dastan. Dastan stared back with wary eyes.

"Nice move, kid," an older boy called out with a laugh. "I'll wager these dates I just found he'll have Hutan on the ground for good within five minutes. Any takers?"

"I'll take that bet," another young street dweller replied. "This chunk of eggplant against your dates."

The wagering among the growing crowd continued, but Dastan paid no attention. He was still watching Hutan and calculating his next move. He couldn't rely on his size—small, but wiry—to overpower his opponent. No, he had to rely on his brains and agility.

"Give up, little Dastan," Hutan said as he

circled warily. "You can't hope to outwrestle me. Why wear yourself out?"

"Nice try, my friend." Dastan skittered to one side as Hutan lunged at him. "But I—"

"There he is!" a new voice rang out, causing both wrestlers to pause.

It was an all too familiar voice.

Dastan glanced over and saw a pair of burly, raggedly dressed youths grinning stupidly as they hurried toward the fighters.

"Titus and Darius," he muttered.

The pair were known as the biggest, nastiest bullies on the streets. Titus was tall and pale with a shifty look. Darius was shorter and hairier than his friend but just as mean. He never went anywhere without his pair of ill-tempered pet vipers.*

The spectators inched back a few steps, their

---

* Dastan had run into these two unsavory characters in *The Chronicle of Young Dastan*.

expressions ranging from curiosity to fear. Even Hutan stepped away from the fight, eyeing the newcomers suspiciously.

Titus swaggered forward, ignoring the others. "We were looking for you, Dastan."

"And we're not the only ones." Darius smirked. One of the vipers was wrapped around his neck, flicking its forked tongue in and out. "Half the city wants to know where you are."

"Really?" Dastan shrugged. "I think you must be confused. Why would anyone care about a common street rat like me?"

"Good question," Titus said. "All we know is the palace guards are on the hunt for a troublemaker who insulted some guests of King Sharaman's. From the description they gave, we're pretty sure that it's you."

"Yeah." Darius was still smirking. "And there's a reward for your capture. A big one!"

Dastan didn't answer. His mind was racing as he realized what this meant.

His latest troubles weren't over.

It had all started when he'd first heard about the Torch of Atar, an ancient relic hidden away long ago. A magical talisman with the power to control light and darkness.

Or so the rumors said. Dastan didn't believe in magic.

But Javed had.

Dastan felt a pang of pain and grief when he thought of Javed. He'd been his only true friend on the streets. Javed had wanted to seek out the Torch, and he'd died because of it.

Despite his friend's convictions, Dastan didn't believe the Torch had any great power. But the White Huns, who were guests of the Persian king, had killed kind and good Javed in their zeal to possess it. Dastan would have done anything to foil their chances of getting the object. So with the help of a new friend, Cyra, and a local Magian named Vindarna, he'd kept the Torch away from the White Huns.*

Now it seemed the White Huns were holding a grudge and were determined to get their hands on him any way they could.

"Are you going to come quietly?" Darius cracked his knuckles, the sound breaking into Dastan's memory. "Or do we have to beat you up and drag you?"

Dastan could guess which the cruel bullies would prefer. "You'll have to catch me first," he taunted.

He jumped away as Darius swung a meaty fist at him. Then he glanced toward the nearest building, calculating the distance to it. If he could get there, he'd be home free. The rooftops of Nasaf were Dastan's kingdom. Nobody

---

* These various events were depicted in *The Chronicle of Young Dastan*.

could catch him up there. His speed had earned him the title of fastest messenger in the city.

"Guess we're finished here," Hutan blurted out, dashing forward. He grabbed the lamb shank and took off.

"Hey!" Dastan protested, darting after him, his hunger outweighing his need to escape.

"Not so fast!" Titus grabbed him by the arm, swinging him around and slamming him against a heap of garbage. Tile shards and bits of stale rice flew everywhere.

"Let go!" Dastan forgot about the lamb as he struggled to break free.

He kicked Titus in the shin. The bully yelped, and his grip loosened.

That was all Dastan needed. He wrenched free and took off.

HISSSSSS!

Something flew through the air and wrapped around his neck. Dastan cried out as he felt scales slither against his skin. Darius's serpent!

"Get off!" he cried, scrabbling to loosen the viper's hold on him.

At that moment he felt the second viper land on his leg. Before he could shake it loose, it zipped around both legs, bringing him down with a thud.

A second later the bullies were on him. One of them—Dastan couldn't see which—kneeled on his back while the other shoved his face into the ground.

"Don't mess up his face too much," Titus ordered. "The guards have to be able to recognize him."

"Guess you're right." Darius sounded disappointed.

Dastan was able to raise his head. He spit out a mouthful of grit. "Let go!" he shouted again.

The bullies ignored him. They hauled him to his feet, keeping both his arms twisted behind his back.

"Let's go find those soldiers," Titus said.

"Yeah." Darius licked his lips. "I can't wait to start spending our reward!"

Dastan struggled as hard as he could. But he might as well have been struggling against Nasaf's city walls. Together, Titus and Darius were just too strong.

The other orphans and assorted street dwellers fell back as the pair pushed him along. For a moment, Dastan dared to hope one of them would help, but he knew it was a foolish wish. Nobody ever stood up to Titus and Darius.

Until . . . "What are you doing to that boy?" a voice rang out. "Let him go at once!"

Dastan was just as surprised as the bullies. All three of them turned to see who had spoken.

It was a man Dastan had never seen before. That was strange enough—Dastan knew just about everyone in this part of the city.

Stranger yet, the man wore the opulent silk robes of an upper-class priest or nobleman. Nobody who dressed like that ever came near this part of the city.

"This is no business of yours," Titus growled at the man. Then he turned and gave his captive another shove.

"This is your last warning," the stranger said, his voice hard. "Unhand him."

Darius snorted. "Get lost, fancy-pants."

Out of the corner of his eye, Dastan saw the stranger make a sudden move with one hand. A second later Darius let out a howl of pain. He let go of Dastan and clamped both hands on the right side of his head.

"My ear!" he yowled. "He cut off my ear!"

CHAPTER TWO

There was a clamor of amazement from the remaining crowd. Darius kept howling with pain and outrage, while Titus grabbed a scrap of soiled fabric off the ground and tried to mop up his friend's blood.

The stranger ignored it all. He stepped toward Dastan. "Are you all right?" he asked.

Dastan stared at him, awed and a little confused. Whoever this man was, he was surely the most skilled of warriors. He'd moved so fast that Dastan hadn't even seen the weapon he'd used against Darius!

"I'm, I'm . . . fine," he stammered. "Uh, I guess I owe you my thanks."

He shot a look over at the bullies. Darius was still clutching his bleeding ear, but he'd finally stop yowling.

"Let's get out of here," Titus muttered to his friend while glaring at Dastan. "We can finish this business later."

Darius shot Dastan an evil look. The blood dripping down his face made him appear even meaner and crazier than usual.

"Yeah," he said. "We'll be back. Then you'll pay."

In response to the threat, the stranger glanced at the bullies. They both started running. Within seconds they had disappeared into the maze of streets and alleyways leading away from the dump.

"Now that they're gone, I'd like to speak with you, Dastan," the man said, turning his attention back to him. "Do you know of someplace we can go that's more private?"

Dastan turned to face him warily. "How did you know my name?" Then a possible answer occurred to him. "Wait—are you a friend of Vindarna's?"

It was the one answer that made sense. The powerful Magian was the only member of the ruling class who knew Dastan by name. Even the shopkeepers who often hired him to carry their messages merely referred to him as "the fast one" or "that scrawny boy from the rooftops."

"Vindarna?" the stranger echoed, a smile flitting briefly over his sun-darkened face. "Yes. That's how I knew your name. I've known Vindarna for many, *many* years. He's the one who suggested I find you."

Dastan remembered what Titus and Darius had said about a reward on his head. Vindarna had helped him once, though Dastan still didn't understand why. Before that, the Magian had always been a mysterious, even frightening, figure that the street rats steered clear of when he wandered into their territory. Could Dastan really trust him? What if he'd sent this man to capture him for the reward?

Dastan decided to err on the side of caution. "Well, it seems you've found me," he said as he led the stranger away from the dump. Now that the excitement was over, most of the other kids had already returned to scrounging for scraps and paid them little attention. "So I must ask, for what purpose did you seek me out?"

He was careful to keep his distance as they stopped at the mouth of a deserted alley. But the stranger made no move to grab him, so Dastan relaxed—slightly—and waited for an answer.

"Much better," the man said, breathing

deeply. "Now that we are away from that awful stench, let me properly introduce myself. My name is Kazem. And it would seem I am in need of a messenger."

"Oh!" Dastan relaxed even more. "Then you've come to the right place."

Kazem held up a hand. "Wait. This is no ordinary job. I need someone fast, someone I can trust, to carry a very important package . . . to Babylon."

"Babylon?" Dastan blinked. "Wait—you mean, *the* Babylon?"

"That's right. I realize it's a slightly longer trip than usual . . ."

Dastan raised an eyebrow. "I can't go to Babylon! How would I even get there?" Then his streetwise eyes narrowed. "You don't expect me to *run* all that way? I mean, I'm fast, but . . ."

Kazem shook his head. "I could set you up with a caravan traveling that way," he explained.

"But why me? Why not just send your package with the caravan?"

"As I said, I need someone I can trust," Kazem replied. "I've heard you're the most reliable messenger in Nasaf. And if Vindarna finds you worthy, well, who am I to argue?"

"But I can't go to Babylon," Dastan repeated. "For one thing, I hear the Babylonians are not especially friendly to Persians. It's said they're unwilling to accept that Babylon is indeed part of the empire despite their many attempts over the years to regain their independence."

Kazem let out a soft chuckle. "You surprise me, my young friend. You know a lot of history for a common street rat."

"I'm full of surprises." Even as he said it Dastan bit his lip, thinking again of Javed. He had been a street rat, too. But that hadn't stopped him from wanting to learn everything he could about the world. If not for his curious friend, Dastan might never have heard of the walled city of Babylon—or most other things outside Nasaf's city limits.

Kazem nodded. "Well then, why not expand your territory? You might even enjoy the adventure. Find more surprises. See new wonders."

Dastan shook his head. Not that long ago he might have been tempted. He'd always dreamed of escaping the gritty dreariness of the streets, perhaps seeing some of the glories of the empire that Javed had told him about. And this job would certainly be an adventure—leaving the familiar surroundings, traveling across the desert, visiting an exotic city . . .

But he wasn't in the mood for more adventure right now. He'd had more than his share lately. And if he had learned anything, it was that wonders and adventures were too often attached to danger—and loss.

"Sorry," he said, shaking his head. "I appreciate what you did for me earlier. And I hope you find someone to carry your package. But I'm not interested."

He started to turn away. Kazem stopped him with a hand on his shoulder.

"Wait," he said. "We haven't discussed the topic of payment...."

Then he named a sum—one so large that Dastan's jaw dropped.

"I'm not finished. That's only the payment up front," Kazem went on. "You'll get twice that amount when you return after completing the job."

Dastan's head spun. Kazem was offering more than just payment for a tough job. It was enough money to get Dastan off the streets once and for all!

For a moment he dared to think what this could mean. He could leave the teeming trash dump behind and become a respectable member of society. What would it be like to have a real home with a real bed, clean clothes, money to buy food whenever he was hungry— or even when he wasn't? He was sure King Sharaman himself couldn't ask for more than that to be content. . . .

"There he is!" someone shouted from farther down the alley.

Dastan spun around. Several of King Sharaman's soldiers had just appeared around a corner. Titus and Darius must have run and fetched them!

"I've got to go," Dastan told Kazem.

He didn't hesitate. Money or not, he wasn't going to stick around and get caught. He leaped toward the nearest wall. It was built of rough brick that would be easy to climb. Once he was up it, he knew the soldiers would have no chance of catching him. Not here on the familiar rooftops surrounding the dump.

"Dastan, wait!"

Kazem grabbed him, pulling him down before he'd climbed more than a few feet. Dastan struggled against his grip.

"Let me go!" he cried in a panic.

"Hush," Kazem murmured. "It will be all right." Then he turned to face the approaching soldiers. "If you're looking for that street rat, I just saw him," he called out to them. "He went that way."

He pointed off to the left. At the same time, he yanked Dastan into a deep doorway to their right.

"Let go!" Dastan hissed, struggling harder than ever. "They'll never fall for that. Titus and Darius already spotted me!"

"Hush," Kazem said again. "Keep quiet and let them pass us by."

Dastan was starting to wonder if Kazem

was soft in the head. How could he think his simple trick could possibly work? All he'd done was trap Dastan in this doorway!

He poked his head out, gauging how long he had to make it out and across the alley to the next rooftop. To his surprise, he was just in time to see the soldiers rush around the next corner to the left!

"This way, boys!" one of the soldiers called to the others. "The man said he went this way!"

"Hurry!" Titus added.

Dastan hardly dared to believe it. "But— but how . . ." he stammered.

"People are easily fooled if you understand how they think," Kazem told him calmly. "But never mind that. Have you thought over my offer?"

Biting his lip, Dastan glanced once more in the direction the soldiers had gone. He was beginning to realize that Nasaf wasn't safe for him right now. Perhaps it *would* be better to take advantage of this timely offer and get out of town for a while.

"All right," he said, turning to face Kazem. "You have yourself a messenger."

CHAPTER THREE

The square near Nasaf's main gate was a bustling place. Street vendors hawked their wares, haggling with shoppers over prices. Newly arrived travelers dusty with desert sand watered their horses and other livestock at the public troughs. Alert, scrawny dogs nosed for scraps in the gutter.

Dastan didn't pay any of it much attention. He was perched on the high balcony of a rug shop behind a row of decorative tiles, keeping an eye on the guards leaning lazily on their weapons beside the huge gate. Nearby, a line of camels dozed and chewed their cud in the shade of an awning. Men swathed in desert robes hurried around tying things to their pack saddles. Dastan figured this had to be the caravan Kazem had mentioned. The man had ordered Dastan to meet him here on the hour, which was now only a few minutes away.

Dastan felt a familiar pang of worry as he contemplated leaving Nasaf, even for a short time. He'd never ventured far from its borders. But what choice did he really have? He was wanted—and not in a good way. And the only people who would miss him were those who might collect the reward on his head. He'd spent the last few hours avoiding everyone he knew, not sure which of his fellow street rats might turn him in for that money. No, he decided anew, the sooner he got out of Nasaf the better.

Again he scanned the crowds for Kazem.

Suddenly a hand grabbed him from behind, closing on his shoulder like a vise.

"Aaah!" he screamed.

Twisting and contorting his body, Dastan managed to free himself. Then he spun around, fists at the ready.

It was Vindarna in his blood red robes.

"Easy, boy." Vindarna peered down his long, thin nose at him. "It's not the Huns come to roast you for their dinner."

"Sorry." Dastan lowered his fists, still wary. "How did you find me up here?"

"I have my ways," Vindarna said, distracted. He was looking all around. Finally, his pale, bony hand emerged clutching a small scrap of parchment. "Here—this is for you."

Dastan glanced at the parchment. Words were scrawled on it, along with a few numbers.

"What is it?" he asked.

Vindarna shot him a sharp look. "I nearly

forgot. You haven't enjoyed the benefits of a proper Persian education, have you?"

"I can read a little," Dastan said defensively. "I taught myself."

Vindarna didn't appear impressed. "It's a note Cyra left with me before she set out for home," he explained. "Directions to her family's farm . . . in case you change your mind about joining her."*

Dastan looked at the parchment again. He'd only known Cyra for a few days, but she was the closest thing he had to a true friend now that Javed was gone.

A flicker of sadness came over Dastan, and he wondered, not for the first time, if he should have gone with her. He shook his head. No—Nasaf would always be his home. Even if it wasn't a very welcoming one at the moment.

---

* At the end of *The Chronicle of Young Dastan* Cyra left Nasaf to be with her family near Bishapur and invited Dastan to join her.

"Thanks," he said, tucking the parchment into his clothes.

"Yes, yes," Vindarna said impatiently. "But that's not why I came. I have important matters to discuss with you."

"Is this about Kazem?" Dastan asked.

"Who?"

"Kazem. He said he was a friend of yours."

"I have no friend by that name," Vindarna said.

"Are you sure?" Dastan asked.

Vindarna shot him a sharp, suspicious look. "Are you doubting my memory or my truthfulness, boy?"

When Vindarna looked at him that way, Dastan remembered why he had always found the Magian an imposing and frightening figure. Vindarna's eyes seemed to bore into his very soul, demanding answers to questions that Dastan couldn't even begin to know.

"Neither," he said quickly. "I doubt neither. It must have been a misunderstanding."

"Who is this man—this Kazem?" Vindarna peered at him more closely than ever. "What did he want with you?"

"Nothing important." Dastan hesitated, wondering if he should tell the Magian about his trip to Babylon. Now that he'd had a chance to think it over it was beginning to seem too good to be true, and Vindarna was said to be one of the wisest men in Nasaf. . . . But looking into the man's glittering black eyes, as cold and distant as those of a serpent, Dastan decided to hold his tongue. "Nothing at all," he went on. "He is merely someone in need of my services as a messenger."

"I see." Vindarna seemed to lose interest immediately. "Fine, fine. I didn't come to discuss trivial matters of messages and addresses. I've received some troubling news. There are rumors flying all over Nasaf that the Skull of the Burnt City has surfaced."

Dastan didn't answer. Angry shouts had just rung out from the square below. Ducking farther behind the tiles, he peered out. Whew! It was only a runaway donkey being chased by its owner. He turned back to Vindarna. "What does that have to do with me?"

"Surely you've heard of the Skull?" Vindarna said. "Or at least the mysterious ruin known as the Burnt City?"

Dastan shook his head. "If it won't help me fill my belly, such chitchat means little to me."

His words came out sounding rather harsh, but he let them stand. He couldn't help being annoyed by Vindarna's intensity. Why would the Magian expect him to care about his rumors and artifacts? The last time Dastan had paid attention to such things, it had done him more harm than good.

If Vindarna noticed Dastan's ire, he gave no indication of it. His deep-set black eyes held a faraway look.

"The Skull is said to have strong and dangerous mystical powers," he said in a low, singsong voice. "If it falls into the wrong hands, it could mean the end of everything."

Dastan rolled his eyes. He'd heard that one before.

"I must find out if the rumors are true," Vindarna went on. "I want you to come with me."

"What?" That got Dastan's attention. "Come with you? Where?"

"I depart for Ardasheer tomorrow at dawn," Vindarna replied. "I don't know where the road shall lead after that—perhaps to the Burnt City itself. Will you come?"

He locked onto Dastan's light eyes with his intense dark ones. Dastan gulped. He owed

Vindarna his life. But that didn't mean he trusted him.

"But—but *why?*" Dastan blurted out. "What help could I possibly be to you? I'm nobody."

The Magian looked away. He was silent for a long moment.

"I'm not so sure about that," he said at last. "There's something about you, Dastan. Something special. I don't know what it is. But all the signs and prophecies point to you being destined to become much more than you are right now. Perhaps even destined for . . . greatness."

Dastan shook his head, his momentary sense of duty toward Vindarna fading. Prophecies, signs? That was nonsense, just like all the silly rumors about the Torch of Atar—and now this mystical skull. He had turned his back on such nonsense. Unless he could hold it in his hands, taste it, or see it, there was no point in believing.

He might be an uneducated street rat, but he wasn't stupid. He already knew what could happen when he got mixed up in one of Vindarna's quests. Besides, why would he set out on a possibly dangerous journey for free when he'd already arranged for one that might pay him enough to get off the streets for good? Once again he allowed himself to dream about what that could mean. A place of his own, a place in the world . . .

"Thanks, but I'll have to pass," he said with a firm nod of his head. "I'm going to be busy tomorrow."

Vindarna frowned. "Dastan, do not be hasty in this decision," he said urgently. "The fate of the world itself . . ."

"Excuse me." Dastan had just spotted Kazem. He was talking to one of the camel handlers. "I've got to go."

He smoothly dodged past Vindarna. Kazem

had already disappeared behind the line of humpbacked animals.

Ignoring Vindarna's almost frantic calls, Dastan swung down from the roof. He took a quick look around for the palace guards, then dashed across the square toward the waiting caravan—and his future.

For endless days, all Dastan had seen was sand. It caked his face, coated his mouth, and worked its way inside his clothes. He'd begun to believe all that was left in the world was sand. But as the camels continued their steady, swinging gait across the desert, the sand finally gave way to patches of scrubby brush and then, finally, to greenery. Soon the landscape was nearly as lush as the gardens behind King Sharaman's palace, with fields of crops as far as the eye could see, interrupted only by the road and an occasional river. The hot, dry air was swallowed up by equally hot, but humid, air, soaking everyone in sticky sweat and making them feel as if they were swimming through honey.

After a day or two of this, a cry finally went up from the front of the caravan. "Babylon is in sight!"

Dastan nearly wept with joy. He'd started to think they might never arrive at their destination. He hurried forward, squinting against the glare of the midday sun. A walled city shimmered on the horizon, rising up out of the ground like a mirage, all exotic towers and soaring spires.

Babylon.

Dastan felt a shiver of awe as he gazed upon the city. Then he remembered why he was there. Reaching down, he touched the small metal box tucked into his waistband. Kazem had made him promise not to open it, though Dastan had been tempted more than once during the long journey. What could be important enough to be worth so much trouble—and so much money?

As soon as the caravan passed through the city gates, Dastan hurried away from the others. Kazem had told him exactly how to reach his destination, and Dastan had committed the directions to memory. He made his way along several busy streets crowded with people wearing colorful and unusual clothes and speaking with lilting foreign accents.

Babylon looked, felt, and even smelled different from Nasaf. The buildings were taller and narrower, their bricks reddish rather than the color of sand, and many of them were decorated with gold and silver accents or with striking mosaics depicting the sun, moon, and stars. Plants and trees grew everywhere, and a riotous array of flowers overflowed the edge of nearly every balcony. The scents of unfamiliar foods and spices drifted along in the moist breeze blowing continuously off the Euphrates River, which bisected the city.

Dastan couldn't help taking it all in as he hurried along, though he did his best to stay focused on his mission. There would be plenty of time for sightseeing later. He planned to start by spending a few coins of the money Kazem had already given him on some of that delicious-smelling Babylonian food.

". . . Through the crooked arch and then to the left," he murmured as he reached another of the landmarks Kazem had mentioned. "Now it's just two more streets and across an open square and down the far alley to the house with the brown door."

He pulled out the metal box as he walked. Once again he wondered what was inside. Now that he was about to give it up, it was harder than ever to resist his own curiosity. What would be the harm in taking a peek?

Just then, he reached the square Kazem had described. A public spice market was set up there, and people wandered among tables piled high with fragrant powders and leaves.

In the center of the square stood several burly men who appeared to be soldiers or guards. They all wore matching uniforms and carried long, curved swords in their belts.

Dastan felt a brief ripple of anxiety as he neared them. Then he remembered. He was in a foreign city, one where the guards had no reason to take any interest in him. Sure enough, they spared him no more than a brief, curious glance as he passed by, perhaps noting his dusty Persian clothing.

His steps slowed as he neared his destination. He turned the corner into the alley and . . .

"Oh!" he gasped.

Two men stood there, one very tall and the

other short and stout. But Dastan barely gave them a glance.

His eyes were locked on something—*someone*—else. Lying broken in the street was the limp body of a broad-shouldered man, a dagger sticking out of his throat.

CHAPTER FOUR

The sight in front of him made Dastan's stomach turn. He'd seen his fair share of violence, but this was unexpected—especially in the lush and seemingly peaceful streets of Babylon. Nothing dark should lurk there. His heart racing, Dastan tried to process the scene.

The man's bloodstained uniform was the same as those worn by the soldiers out in the square. He appeared to be dead, though Dastan didn't get a good look before the other men spotted him.

"Hello!" the short one said in the familiar dialect of Nasaf and the surrounding areas. He smiled, his round cheeks as rosy as a baby's. "You must be Dastan."

Dastan was taken aback. "You—I—what happened here?" he stammered in a shaky voice.

"Don't know." The taller man had a gruff, guttural voice and heavy brows that cast a shadow over his eyes. "Must've met up with some trouble."

"Yes, we were just about to report it to the proper authorities. By the way, I'm Babak and this is Murdad." The shorter man waved a hand at his companion. "We were expecting you."

"You're Kazem's friends?" Dastan felt a flash of suspicion at the coincidence. Then he glanced past the men, realizing that the brown door he was looking for was right there at the end of the alley, and he relaxed. "I brought this for you," he told them.

He held out the box, but Babak brushed it aside. "Later," he said, smiling ruefully. "First let's tell someone about this poor unfortunate soldier."

Dastan nodded, relieved that his first impression had clearly been mistaken. These men hadn't killed that soldier. They'd merely happened across his body, just as Dastan had.

"I passed some soldiers out in the square," he offered. "We could alert them."

"Fine idea, my boy. Lead the way, if you please." Babak swept a hand before him.

Dastan hurried ahead, still clutching the metal box. When he emerged into the square, he saw that the soldiers had not moved. He hurried toward them.

"Excuse me," he called out. "There's been some—*oof!*"

Someone had bumped him from behind,

hard enough to send him lurching forward. The box flew out of his grip as he threw both hands out to break his fall.

CLANG! The box hit the ground and popped open. "Urf!" Dastan grunted as he skidded across the hard-packed ground. The pouch he'd tucked into his clothes came loose and burst open, releasing a rain of coins onto the street, along with a crust of bread and a few other items he'd been carrying.

But Dastan's focus was on the money, the first part of his payment from Kazem. He jumped to his feet. Even now, the soldiers and passersby were hurrying closer. Any of them could steal his hard-earned payment! "You all right, son?" one of the soldiers asked.

"I'm fine." Dastan grabbed a handful of silver coins and tucked them into his pouch. He noticed the metal box lying where it had fallen. Another soldier was peering down at its scattered contents, which mostly seemed to be pieces of parchment with writing on them.

Dastan glanced back, wondering why Babak and Murdad weren't gathering up their precious box and its contents. But they were nowhere in sight.

That was weird. But Dastan had little time to ponder as he fished another coin out of a crack in the street and a few more from nearby. Meanwhile, the second soldier had just grabbed one of the larger papers that had fallen on the ground. He scanned it. Then his cheeks began to grow redder and redder.

"Seize him!" he shouted suddenly, waving the paper. "You, Persian boy, you're under arrest!"

"What?" Dastan blurted out, glancing up, his hand on another coin.

The other soldier looked startled. He

grabbed Dastan by the arm so hard that the coin flew out of his grasp.

"Come with me, boy," the soldier growled.

Acting on instinct, Dastan twisted his arm and let his lightweight outer traveling robe smoothly slip off.

"Hey!" the soldier yelled when he found himself holding nothing but a handful of linen. Dastan was already several yards away.

Soldiers were coming at him from all directions, hands on their swords. Dastan crouched down—then leaped directly at one of the soldiers. The man raised his arm to fend off Dastan, who then grabbed the soldier's arm with both hands, flinging himself upward and doing a flip right over the man's head!

"Stop him!" one of the others shouted.

But it was too late. Dastan dodged a few bystanders, leaping over a table piled high with mounds of cinnamon. His foot trailed through one, causing a fragrant cloud to hover in the air.

The cries of the spice merchant mingled with those of the soldiers. Dastan didn't look back. He raced toward the nearest building. Grabbing a window ledge, he scrambled up onto the edge of a low roof.

Only then did he finally risk a glance behind him. One soldier was gathering up the box and its contents. The others, looking angry, were coming fast.

"Get down from there!" the biggest one yelled.

Dastan didn't answer. He was focused on the crowd of people scrambling to grab the rest of his money off the street. His heart sank as his dreams of respectability and comfort faded. He'd be lucky if the few coins he'd managed to retrieve would pay his way back to Nasaf. And as he hadn't delivered the package, there'd be no more money waiting for him there.

But he'd grown used to disappointment and hardship. Why should he expect anything different now? Unless . . . he could somehow get the package *back* from the soldiers.

He'd have to deal with that later. Turning away, he sprinted up the steeply pitched roof, then raced along its peak. At the far end, he flung himself across a narrow alley and onto the next rooftop, which was made of rounded polished stone. His bare feet slipped, and he fell and skidded downward before he could catch himself.

"Aaaaah!" he cried, his fingers scraping painfully as he dug for a hold.

But it was no good. His fingers slid off into thin air, and Dastan went flying. Twisting his body around, his eyes widened when he saw that he was heading straight toward the trunk of a large palm tree.

"*Oof!*" he grunted as he hit it. The breath

flew out of his body, but he acted on instinct, wrapping both arms around the rough wood of the tree trunk. He felt his already tattered clothes rip even more as he slid down the trunk, but he swung both feet up and dug in with his toes, finally stopping his downward momentum.

Whew! He hung there for a moment, panting. Then he looked around. He was in a courtyard garden packed with lush fruit trees.

Dastan let himself slide more slowly down the trunk to the ground. For a second he didn't think there was any way out other than the barred doorway leading into the adjoining house.

Then he spotted a single slender archway. Hurrying over, he peered out on to a quiet, narrow street lined with arched entrances that led into similar gardens.

There was no sign of his pursuers, though he

could hear faint shouts in the distance. "Since I don't have much money anymore, might as well find a quick meal here on my way out," he murmured to himself, ducking back into the garden and looking around. Spying a plum tree nearby, he hurried over and grabbed one of the plump fruits, shoving it into his mouth. It was the sweetest thing he'd ever tasted. As the juice dripped down his chin, he reached for another.

He jumped as a sudden loud screech erupted into his ear. A second later something landed on his shoulder, and then sharp claws dug into his skin.

"Aaaah!" he cried, leaping away and shoving whatever it was that had attacked him.

The screech came again. The second plum was plucked out of his hand, and a moment later the weight left his shoulder. Dastan staggered back, staring at the large, grayish brown monkey that had just landed in the lower branches of the plum tree.

"You!" Dastan cried accusingly, clutching his throbbing shoulder. "You scared me half to death!"

The monkey chittered irritably, then turned away, nibbling at the plum. Dastan rolled his eyes and reached for another fruit. Before his hand could close over it, the monkey spun around and let out a warning screech.

"Okay, okay!" Dastan held up both hands and backed away. "I get it. Your fruit. Not mine. I guess even the monkeys here don't care for Persians. . . ."

He turned and hurried toward the archway. This time when he looked out, he gulped. A Babylonian soldier had just rounded the corner at the far end of the street.

"Uh-oh," Dastan muttered, shooting a look around.

Back in Nasaf, he knew every rooftop escape

route within a mile of the dump. But this wasn't Nasaf. This was Babylon. And *this* city was completely foreign to him in every way.

Still, he didn't want to get trapped in the garden. He would have to take his chances on the rooftops. Dashing out and across the narrow street, he swung up onto the next building. Behind him, he heard the soldier let out a shout. Several other shouts answered him, seeming to come from every direction.

Dastan gulped and sprinted across the roof. He did a forward flip across another narrow alley, landing on a balcony and then scrambling upward. Then he paused to listen and catch his breath. How long would it take his pursuers to catch up?

It didn't matter. Staying around to find out was a bad idea. He glanced down into the next alley. Someone had hung some laundry there to dry. That was his way out!

Dastan dropped lightly to the ground. When he examined the laundry, he saw that he was in luck. Among the clothes were some robes about his size, though they were far more opulent than anything he'd ever worn before.

He chose a robe of the softest indigo cotton and slipped it on over his rags. The luxurious fabric felt strange against his skin.

Grabbing another piece of fabric, he wrapped it around his head, pulling it down as far as he could to hide his features. Then he darted to the end of the alley, no longer looking like a Persian street rat. If he could blend in as a Babylonian, perhaps he could escape the city before the soldiers found him.

He darted out into the street. But he was so busy watching for soldiers that he didn't pay enough attention to where he was going. When a boy around his own age stepped out of a doorway, Dastan crashed into him hard enough to send them both reeling.

"Yow!" Dastan blurted out in surprise.

"Excuse me," the boy said at the same time.

He was dressed in pale Babylonian robes, but his accent was as Persian as Dastan's own. Dark curls poked out from beneath his turban, and his large, intelligent brown eyes were rimmed by long lashes.

"Who are you?" the boy asked, looking confused. "And why are you wearing Bhimji's sister's favorite robe?"

"I— I— What?" Dastan stammered, his eyes darting from his now obviously girly clothing to the street, and then back again. "This is my robe. So, um, if you'll pardon me . . ."

He tried to push past, but the boy blocked his way. "I'd know that robe anywhere," he insisted. "I recognize the small tear on the hem where a goat nibbled at it." He laughed. "You see, Bhimji and I thought it would be funny if we dipped the hem in quince jelly, and sure enough . . ."

Dastan barely heard him. Several soldiers had just raced around the corner at one end of the street. He spun, ready to run in the opposite direction.

But it was too late. More soldiers were pouring into view at that end of the block as well.

Dastan froze. He was surrounded!

CHAPTER FIVE

"Where'd he go?" one of the soldiers shouted.

"There!" Another pointed straight at Dastan. "Isn't that him?"

Dastan tensed and balled his fists. This appeared to be the end.

"What's going on here?" The boy in the light-colored robes spoke up.

Dastan had almost forgotten about him. He shot the stranger a look.

The soldiers skidded to a stop. "Step aside," one of them told the other boy. "This Persian rascal is wanted for crimes against Babylon, including the murder of a member of the royal guard."

"Persian?" The strange boy laughed. "Surely you're mistaken! The only Persian here is me. Anyone can see that this is Jaiji, sister of my friend and fellow student Bhimji and daughter of the high priest Manaksha, master of my school. As I'm certain you're aware, Manaksha recently presided over the first official state visit of the child princess Tamina of the holy city of Alamut!"

A soldier peered into Dastan's face. "No disrespect intended, young man," he told the boy. "But I'm quite sure this is no Babylonian girl at all, but rather the very *boy* we want. He has changed his clothes somehow, perhaps through some Persian sorcery, but I recognize his conniving face."

The boy raised an eyebrow. "I see," he said in an amused voice. "Well, you can take her into custody, I suppose. But Jaiji's father will surely have something to say about it when he finds out."

That seemed to give the soldiers pause. They exchanged worried glances. But the first soldier still looked suspicious.

"If this is truly your Babylonian friend and not a common street rat, let her prove it," he said.

"Certainly. Go ahead, Jaiji." The boy turned toward Dastan and winked.

Dastan wasn't sure how to react. What was this stranger doing? The moment Dastan opened his mouth it would be clear that he was Persian—and a boy.

He gulped, opened his mouth, and . . . to his surprise, heard a high-pitched voice. It appeared to be coming from his own lips, though he hadn't spoken a word!

The voice recited a complex prayer Dastan

had never heard before. And, it was in a flawless Babylonian dialect!

The guards were equally startled. They immediately bowed their heads and murmured apologies.

"Sorry for the confusion, young lady," one said to Dastan. "I hope you won't see a need to mention this to your esteemed father."

As the soldiers backed off, the other boy grabbed Dastan's arm and dragged him into a nearby building. Seconds later, they were alone in a dim, dusty, echoing hallway.

"Wait. Wh— What just happened?" Dastan stammered. "Who are you?"

The other boy grinned. "I wasn't sure it would work," he said, his brown eyes dancing with glee. He seemed completely unbothered by the events that had just occurred or by Dastan's potential status as an outlaw. "I've been practicing, but still . . ."

"Practicing what? I don't understand." Dastan glanced around, feeling trapped in the windowless hall. "Where did that voice come from?"

"It was me—I threw my voice to make the guards think you were speaking." The stranger's grin broadened. "My Babylonian accent is pretty good, eh?"

Dastan shook his head. "Threw your voice? How?"

The other boy shrugged nonchalantly. "Just a little magic trick I learned from one of my schoolmates."

"There's no such thing as magic," Dastan muttered. "However, you were quite convincing as a girl." He slid closer to the door, peering out to see if the soldiers had left.

"By the way, my name's Ghalander," the other boy said, undeterred. "I came from Ctesiphon to study religion and astronomy and become a scribe. You're Persian, too, right? What's your name?"

"Dastan."

"Nice to meet you, Dastan," Ghalander said cheerfully. "So why were those soldiers chasing you?"

"Long story." Dastan saw no sign of the soldiers outside. He sidled a little farther into the vestibule.

"Wait, where are you going?" Ghalander hurried to catch up. "If you really have committed some heinous crime, I'll have to turn you in, of course. But I want to hear your side of the story first." He shook his head and his expression grew somber. "I know as well as anyone that the Babylonian guards can be touchy about Persians. And you have an honorable look to you, Dastan."

Dastan tightened his lips in amusement. Honorable? This boy was clearly out of his head.

"Look, I appreciate what you did out there," he said. "But you'll just have to trust it was the right thing. I don't have time to explain. I need to get out of here. There's something I have to find."

Ghalander looked troubled. As Dastan took another step toward the door, he blocked his path.

"I'm afraid I must insist," Ghalander said in a calm but suddenly determined voice. "I cannot allow a criminal to simply walk free without any attempt to stop him if he truly is bad."

"I'm afraid you have no choice," Dastan said. He pushed past Ghalander, heading for the door.

He was almost free. . . .

An instant later he found himself on the ground staring up into Ghalander's calm face, the boy's foot on his chest.

"Now," Ghalander said, only slightly out of breath. "Will you please tell me the truth?"

CHAPTER SIX

What had just happened? Somehow this mild-looking boy had dodged Dastan's shove and then flipped him over onto his back! All within a split second.

That was what Dastan got for letting his guard down. It wouldn't happen again.

"Out of my way," Dastan said, getting to his feet. He darted to one side, putting a shoulder forward to ram past the other boy.

But Ghalander simply caught him by the shoulder and, once more, Dastan saw the world turn upside down.

"*Oof!*" Again he was flat on his back on the floor. "How'd you do that?" he complained when Ghalander's face peered down at him.

"Just a hobby of mine," Ghalander said, waving a hand as though he'd just done something as simple as picking up a stone. "I enjoy studying the martial arts of the eastern lands."

"You seem to have a lot of strange hobbies," Dastan grumbled. He rolled over and sprang to his feet again.

Ghalander stayed where he was. He looked as relaxed and calm as ever. But his legs were spread, his knees slightly bent, and both hands were held at the ready.

"All right," he said. "Are you ready to answer my question yet, Dastan?"

Dastan frowned, rubbing his hip, which had hit the hard floor. He realized he had only two choices. He could grab a brick or stone, call upon all his street smarts and agility, and fight his way past Ghalander in earnest. Or, he could accept defeat gracefully and tell the other boy what he wanted to know.

Looking into Ghalander's serious brown eyes, Dastan's shoulders slumped. There was no choice really.

Besides, Ghalander might be of more use to him as a friend. Dastan certainly didn't need any more enemies in Babylon.

"Fine," he said. "But let's go somewhere more private in case those guards return."

Ghalander smiled, revealing deep dimples in both cheeks. "Come this way."

Dastan followed the other boy down the hallway, still not sure he was doing the right thing. He was used to being alone, relying only on himself. Still, Ghalander was clearly an intelligent boy, not to mention much more physically capable than he seemed at first glance. Maybe he could help Dastan figure out how to make his escape from Babylon.

Soon the two of them were in a small, deserted room near the back of the building. Dastan was relieved to see several high windows that could provide escape if necessary.

"We should be safe here," Ghalander said. "This section of the school is hardly used." He perched on the edge of a table and smiled. "Now go ahead, Dastan. I'm eager to hear your tale."

"All right, this might sound a little wild," Dastan said. "But it all started when a stranger approached me back in Nasaf . . ."

He told the whole story. His first meeting with Kazem. The caravan across the desert. That murdered soldier. The spilled contents of the box. The parchments that were now in the possession of Babylonian soldiers.

Ghalander listened carefully through it

all. "It sounds as if your friends Babak and Murdad were not really your friends at all," he commented when Dastan had finished.

Dastan nodded. Now that he finally had time to stop and think, he realized it must have been one of the pair who'd shoved him and caused the metal box to fall. They must have known that the box's contents would incriminate him, so they had left him to the soldiers and run away. But did that mean he was never supposed to deliver the package to them—or return to Nasaf for the rest of his reward? Had Kazem set him up?

He scowled, angry with himself. The box was as good as gone. "I can't believe I allowed them to trick me like that," he muttered.

"Do not blame yourself," Ghalander said. "There is no shame in being honest and expecting the same from others."

Dastan had nearly forgotten that the other

boy was there. He shot Ghalander a look. "You believe me, then?" he asked.

"Of course," Ghalander said with a shrug. "Why would I not? Now I'm very glad I stepped in to help."

Dastan nodded, glancing at the windows. He was feeling restless again. He didn't know why Kazem, if it was him behind this, and the others wanted him captured, but he didn't plan to make it easy for them. He could get out of the city now and hide out and wait for the next caravan heading back to Nasaf. If he was going to be forced to live on the run, he might as well do it where he knew the lay of the land.

"I thank you for your help," he told Ghalander. "But I'd better be going. I need to get out of Babylon before those soldiers find me again."

"Get *out* of Babylon?" Ghalander laughed. "How do you propose to do that? This is a walled city, and the guards will be watching for you."

Dastan shrugged. "I'll find a way. If the gates are guarded, perhaps I can swim out along the river."

Ghalander looked dubious. "The river's passage is blocked by strong metal grates. There is no easy way out of Babylon."

"What choice do I have but to try?" Dastan retorted. "I can't stay here and wait for them to find me."

"I understand," Ghalander said. "But if we approach this problem rationally, surely we'll discover a solution."

Dastan bit back a sigh. He could tell that Ghalander meant well. But he had no idea what it was like to be in Dastan's skin. And how could he? An educated, highborn boy such as Ghalander had almost nothing in common with a lowly street rat.

"Exactly what do you propose?" Dastan asked with more than a touch of bitterness.

"First," Ghalander said, "we should try to figure out exactly what terrible crimes you are suspected of and why. In that way, perhaps we can go to the authorities and clear up this obvious misunderstanding."

Dastan hesitated. He *was* curious about why these strangers wanted to harm him. If Ghalander really thought he could find some answers...

"I suppose it's worth a try," he said at last. "At least in the hours before sundown, after which I might have a better chance of sneaking past the guards at the gate."

Ghalander smiled. "Good," he said. "Let me help you find a boy's robe to change into and retie your turban in the Babylonian style. Then we'll see what we can find out."

* * *

"Attention, citizens of Babylon!" a voice rang out.

Dastan and Ghalander were approaching one of Babylon's main squares through the city's perplexing maze of streets. Ghalander wanted to seek out some friends who always knew all the gossip around town. He was sure they would be aware of the accusations against Dastan.

"What do you suppose that's about?" Dastan asked as the voice called for attention again.

"Let's find out." Ghalander hurried forward.

Dastan followed, glancing around uneasily. When he'd first arrived in Babylon, the lush greenery lining the streets had seemed beautiful and refreshing. But now Dastan found it claustrophobic, as if every view and possible escape route were obscured by leaves, flowers, or fronds.

A uniformed soldier stood in the middle

of the square. "Attention!" he repeated loudly. "Be warned that a dangerous criminal is in our midst, wanted for murder and sedition. A Persian boy from the desert lands to the east, with light eyes and a shifty look . . ."

As a crowd gathered around the soldier, he went on to describe Dastan in some detail. Even hidden beneath his flowing Babylonian robes and elaborate headdress, Dastan felt exposed.

"Let's go," he hissed, ducking behind a potted citrus tree and dragging Ghalander with him.

"Wait," Ghalander said. "This is what we wanted. Information."

"Be further warned that this Persian troublemaker is very dangerous," the soldier was saying. "He is suspected in several deaths, including that of a member of the Babylonian guard."

The crowd gasped in horror. Dastan

grimaced. Why were they spreading such vicious lies?

"There is a reward for information leading to this scoundrel's capture," the guard finished grimly. "And rest assured, as soon as he is in our custody, he'll be paying for his crimes by being banished to the Valley of the Slaves—forever!"

CHAPTER SEVEN

Dastan couldn't stand to hear any more. None of this made sense. How could he be implicated in such terrible things? And more importantly, who was setting him up?

Horrible images of the Valley of the Slaves danced through his head. He'd heard many rumors of the desolate salt mine where prisoners were forced to toil beneath the hot desert sun until they dropped. It was a place feared by all. There was no way he ever wanted to see it in person. He had to find a way out of town—now.

He turned and darted around the next corner. "Wait!" Ghalander called.

Dastan ignored him, sprinting into an alley. The flowing robes tangled around his legs, slowing him a little as he dashed down one narrow street after another, and he had the urge to rip them off—disguise or no. But before long he'd left the square—and Ghalander's cries—far behind.

Only when he reached the bank of the Euphrates River did he stop to catch his breath. He stared into the murky water, realizing that he was on his own again, and that it was perhaps better that way. Why drag innocent Ghalander into this? Especially when he probably didn't realize how dangerous knowing Dastan could be?

Dastan spent the rest of the afternoon hiding out in a public garden, leaving the shelter of the trees only at dusk. Few people glanced in his direction as he made his way toward the main gates. Still, he felt all too exposed.

When he reached the main gate, his heart sank. The square was swarming with guards. Several stood at attention on either side of the enormous gate, while others moved around methodically, casting an eagle eye on anyone who passed. Still more soldiers patrolled the top of the high, fortresslike city wall.

Ghalander was right. It wasn't going to be easy to breach Babylon's defenses.

Glancing around, Dastan spotted a ramshackle storefront that appeared to be abandoned. Halfway up its tall, narrow façade was a small balcony overlooking the gate. He waited until he was sure nobody was looking, then he shimmied up onto the balcony.

He huddled behind its low stucco wall and settled down to wait.

* * *

Dastan remained in his hiding spot all night and well into the next day. He dozed fitfully a few times, awakening each time hotter, hungrier, and thirstier than before. The scene below did not change. A well-guarded gate—and little hope of escape.

On the second day, the sun climbed high into the sky and then began its descent toward the horizon. Dastan was beginning to despair. Would he never find a way out?

He dozed off again, slipping into frenzied dreams involving running and shouting.

Suddenly he came awake. He sat up with a start as he realized the noise he heard was coming from the square below.

Peering over the edge of the balcony, he saw the gate standing open. Guards were milling around, shouting for people to clear the way. A moment later an exhausted-looking camel staggered in, followed by another, and then a third.

A caravan! This was his chance! If he could take advantage of the commotion and get past the guards, he might be able to slip out through the open gates.

He made his way down and was soon mingling with the crowds gathered to greet the travelers. Beyond the weary camels still trudging through the gates, Dastan could see the open farmland outside beckoning. It was less than a day's walk to a sleepy caravansary he remembered passing on the way here. From there, he could surely find his way back to Nasaf with another caravan. Then he could track down Kazem and find out why Babak and Murdad had tried to have him captured. Perhaps he would discover it had all been a misunderstanding; perhaps Kazem would apologize and pay him the rest of his money, after all. . . .

Dastan sighed and shook his head. Whatever else he might be, he wasn't naïve. And the past two days had given him plenty of time to think. If there was a plot against him, Kazem was certainly involved. Until Dastan knew why, maybe it would be better to stay away from him. Perhaps he should go visit Cyra instead—give things a chance to settle down in Nasaf before he returned. Pleased by the idea, he stuck a hand into his clothes, fishing inside the pouch that held the parchment with the directions to Cyra's home.

But it was nowhere to be found. That was when he remembered that most of what he'd tucked into his clothes had scattered when he'd fallen in the market square. He'd been forced to abandon far too much of his money along with that mysterious box, and he'd given little thought to anything else in his possession when the guards tried to grab him. Cyra's address must have been among the items lost.

"How many more?" a guard shouted at one of the caravaners, jarring Dastan.

"Three more camels," the man replied, wiping the grit from his eyes as he glanced back.

Dastan had to act fast, or he'd miss his chance.

Scooting past the nearest guard, he pressed up against the flank of one of the camels. The animal's rider glanced down in surprise, but Dastan didn't stay there for long. He ducked between the camel's legs and kept moving, working his way toward the gate.

He was almost there. . . . He zipped between two more camels, doing his best to keep out of the guards' sight. The gate was only ten yards away, then five . . .

"It's that Persian murderer!" someone shouted above the hubbub of the caravan.

"Stop him! He's getting away!"

Dastan froze halfway through the massive gate. Glancing back, he saw Babak racing toward him, his round, ruddy face twisted with anger!

"Stop him!" Babak howled.

The guards were already responding. Several came running, pushing past confused caravaners and their camels.

Dastan spun around, realizing he had only a split second to decide what to do. The sprawling green farmland lay before him, with nothing stopping him from reaching it.

But then what? The open fields stretched out for miles in every direction, flat and featureless, offering few places to hide. A man riding a horse or camel would catch him within moments no matter how fast he ran.

Even so, it was tempting. Dastan glanced beyond the gate, longing to be free of this city.

But there was only one real choice. He dashed back into Babylon, zigzagging his way among the camels to give himself a head start.

Moments later he was on the rooftops, moving at top speed as his pursuers' angry voices grew faint behind him.

CHAPTER EIGHT

Dastan didn't stop until he was sure he'd left the soldiers far behind. Even then he didn't feel safe. How long would it take them to find him again?

Ghalander had told him there were other, smaller gates leading out of the city. Dastan made his way to the wall and walked along it in search of the next gate, not wanting to spend another minute in Babylon if he could help it.

When he found the next gate, his heart sank. Murdad was standing in front of it talking to the guards!

Dastan hid behind a wall and watched, his head spinning. If his enemies had warned the guards at two of the gates, surely they'd done so at all of them. With growing concern, Dastan slipped away from the second gate and made his way back into the heart of the city. It seemed there was only one place left to turn. Luckily, he was pretty sure he remembered the route back to Ghalander's school.

As he walked, keeping his head down to avoid eye contact with passersby, Dastan wondered if he was making a fatal error. He'd chosen to trust all the wrong people so far on this adventure—Kazem, Babak, and Murdad. Even Vindarna might have been involved somehow. Would Ghalander betray him, too? Would he never find a friend as loyal as Javed had been? Was his life destined to be a solitary one?

Thinking of Ghalander's open, curious face,

Dastan couldn't fully believe that. It wasn't easy for him to trust anyone since Javed had died. But he needed to believe that Ghalander was truly an ally, or he would have no hope at all.

When he reached the school, the street was bustling with activity. Students poured in and out of the building, shouting to one another and trading cheerful insults. Pedestrians hurried by. Donkeys pulled carts loaded with goods, and a woman ushered a small herd of goats along.

Dastan found a hiding place in an alley across the street. Then he settled down to wait again.

Several hours after dark, the street was finally quiet. Dastan crept over and climbed the rough brick walls of the school building, peering into one window after another. There was a bright moon, allowing him to see fairly well.

The first few rooms he came to were empty.

But finally he found one where a dozen boys lay sound asleep on narrow wooden beds. Among them Dastan spotted Ghalander's familiar face.

Somersaulting gracefully through the window, Dastan landed softly and tiptoed over to Ghalander's bed near the center of the room. He stood there for a moment, staring down at the other boy's sleeping face as soft snores rose and fell around him. He felt torn by his own natural suspicion, honed by years of living by his wits on the streets.

Then he took a deep breath . . . and reached down to touch Ghalander on the shoulder. Ghalander's eyes flew open, and he looked up at Dastan.

"Aaaaaaaaah!" Ghalander shouted at the top of his lungs.

Dastan spun around. The window was too far away to reach in time. Instead he dove under the nearest bed.

He regretted it almost instantly. At least he might have been able to fight his way back to the window. Under here, he had no chance.

But it was too late. He could already hear the other boys coming awake with groans and complaints. Feeling doomed, he huddled there and waited to feel rough hands grab his ankles and drag him out.

"What's all the noise?" a sleepy-sounding voice complained in a strong Babylonian accent.

"I just managed to drift off," someone else grumbled.

"Sorry." Ghalander spoke up, sounding sheepish. "I had a nightmare."

Dastan felt himself relax a little.

There were more grumbles from the other boys. "Try to keep your nightmares to yourself, would you?" one of them moaned. "I need my rest."

The others added a few more complaints

as well. But they soon quieted down. Then, once again, the only sounds in the room were the boy's snores.

The soft padding of bare feet followed, and Ghalander's face appeared in the space below the bed where Dastan was hiding. He gestured for Dastan to come out.

Dastan scooted out and jumped to his feet. Feeling nervous and exposed, he glanced around at the still forms of the other boys.

Ghalander was tiptoeing toward the door, waving for Dastan to come with him. Dastan followed him through another room and up a flight of stairs, finally stopping in a large space that appeared to be some kind of lecture hall.

"I think we're safe here," he said softly, turning to face Dastan. "Sorry about before. You startled me."

Dastan nodded, glancing around. He recognized the paraphernalia of higher learning—parchments, scientific equipment, a globe—though of course he'd never had the advantage of such an education himself. What would it be like to have no greater concerns in a day than learning arithmetic and astronomy or practicing his riding or shooting?

"I'm glad you came back," Ghalander said, breaking into his thoughts. "I heard about what happened at the gate earlier when you tried to sneak out past the caravan."

"You did?" Dastan grimaced. "News travels fast in Babylon."

Ghalander chuckled. "I told you, some of my acquaintances make a point of keeping up with the latest gossip. They also tell me your friends Babak and Murdad are strangers in Babylon themselves."

"I could have told you that," Dastan said. "Their accents give them away as Persians."

"True enough," Ghalander agreed. "In any

case, it seems they arrived only within the past few weeks. Nobody knows who they are or what their business here might be."

Dastan stepped over to a window, looking out over the sleeping city. It was a beautiful place. But to him, it felt like a prison.

"Their business appears to be getting me banished to the Valley of the Slaves," he said, voicing his beliefs aloud for the first time.

"Indeed. It would seem so." Ghalander looked troubled. "I still wasn't able to learn why. But I did manage to find out where they're staying."

Dastan turned to face him, realizing this could be his only chance to find out the truth—and perhaps clear his name. "Take me there," he said.

CHAPTER NINE

"Stay here," Dastan murmured. "I'll go up alone."

"But I want to come!" Ghalander protested in a whisper.

Dastan shook his head. He glanced up at the tall, narrow house rising above them. Ghalander had brought him halfway across the city to this alley near Babylon's eastern wall. It was well past midnight, and the only sounds were the muffled barking of a dog inside one of the buildings and the distant cries of the guards patrolling the top of the wall.

"You've done enough," Dastan told Ghalander. "It's safer for both of us if you stay here and stand guard."

Before the other boy could protest, Dastan grabbed onto the lowest windowsill and swung himself upward, hooking his toes on a protruding brick. From there it was an easy climb to the third floor window Ghalander had pointed out.

Dastan found himself looking into a small, square room. There were no lamps lit, leaving the far corners shadowy and dark. He slid inside and held his breath, waiting.

Nothing happened. The place appeared to be deserted.

Dastan padded around looking for clues— anything that might tell him why his enemies had lured him all the way to Babylon only to try to have him banished to the Valley of the Slaves. There was a table in the middle of the room. Dozens of pieces of parchment were scattered across it. The size and texture of the papers made it clear that they were not the same as those in the box. The remains of two hearty meals sat atop the parchment, the lingering scents of meat and bread making Dastan's stomach grumble.

He ignored his hunger, pushing aside plates and knives and bits of well-gnawed bone. Then he started shuffling through the papers. Enough moonlight came in through the window to show that writing covered most of the bits of parchment. But Dastan only recognized a few words—*Nasaf, desert, king*. Biting his lip in frustration, he picked up one of the pages and stared at it, willing himself to understand the incomprehensible scribbles.

THUMP!

He spun around at the sudden noise from behind him. His heartbeat slowed when he realized it was only Ghalander. "I told you to stay outside!" Dastan hissed.

He shot a nervous look at the closed door on the far wall. What if someone had heard?

"I couldn't resist," Ghalander whispered as he climbed to his feet. "Did you find anything?"

Dastan shrugged. "Just these pieces of parchment."

"What do they say?"

"I don't know." Dastan frowned.

Ghalander gave him a surprised look. "Oh, right," he said. "Here, let me have a look."

He hurried over and began sorting through the papers, tossing aside a few that he said were merely bills or other boring things. "Aha," he said, grabbing a larger page. "Here we go."

"What?" Dastan tossed another anxious glance at the door. "What does it say?"

Ghalander's lips moved silently as he scanned the paper. "It's written in a sloppy hand that's a bit hard to make out," he said. "But it seems to be a letter to Babak from Kazem."

"That's him! The man I told you about." Dastan peered over Ghalander's shoulder. "What does the letter say?"

"It mentions you." Ghalander glanced at him, looking troubled. "As I said, it's a bit hard to read. But from what I can tell, it seems Babak and Murdad are indeed in cahoots with Kazem, all of them hoping to cause your death or banishment."

Dastan nodded grimly. He had suspected it, but it was troubling to have the news confirmed. Why would three grown men go to so much trouble to cause him harm?

"Keep reading," he urged.

"I'm trying." Ghalander scanned the parchment again, his eyes squinting as he tried to decipher the messy hand. "There's something about a prophecy, a journey to a foreign land, and an ancient relic with supernatural powers . . ."

Dastan rolled his eyes. "Don't tell me that's what all this is about," he muttered, grabbing another bit of parchment himself. "I've had enough of so-called supernatural powers to last me a lifetime." He glanced at the scrap he was holding and blinked. "Hang on, what's this?"

"That one appears to contain little more than an address," Ghalander said, glancing over at it. "Someone named Cyra. Think it's another clue?"

"No," Dastan said in surprise. "I know what this is. It's the address of a friend of mine—I brought it with me to Babylon. It came out of my clothes when I fell, and I figured the guards must've picked it up. I wonder how these two ended up with it."

He felt uneasy at the thought that these two men might be more powerful than they appeared and even more uneasy when he realized that Cyra's address had been in their possession. Why would they bother to keep something like that if not to use it at a later date?

"Your friend lives near Bishapur, I see," Ghalander said, looking more closely at the parchment. "That's a nice area; I know it well. My uncle lives very close to there."

"Never mind that." Dastan tucked Cyra's address away, then returned his attention to the other papers. "Do you see anything else that might tell us something useful?"

"I'm looking." Ghalander returned to pawing through the parchments.

Feeling impatient, Dastan prowled around the room, his mind racing. None of this made sense. And why did he seem incapable of escaping silly prophecies? *

---

* A prophecy was foretold in *The Chronicle of Young Dastan* which Vindarna believed had something to do with Dastan.

"Here's something," Ghalander said. "Do you know someone named Vindarna?"

"Yes! Why?" Dastan spun, surprised. As he did, his elbow hit something behind him, and there was a sudden rustle of feathers.

He glanced back and found a pair of round amber eyes staring at him. A falcon! It had been perched in this dark corner all along, sleeping—or perhaps watching them.

Dastan stepped away quickly. But it was too late. The bird let out a sudden shrill cry, causing Ghalander to jump in surprise.

"What was that?" he exclaimed in too loud a voice.

"Hush!" Dastan hissed.

But he knew it didn't matter. The falcon's call must have awakened everyone in the building.

"We've got to get out of here," Dastan whispered, grabbing Ghalander by the arm.

"Just one more second," Ghalander said. "I

want to read the rest of this one...."

"No!" Dastan ripped the parchment out of the other boy's hand, then shoved him toward the window. "Go—now!"

The sounds of sleepy voices drifted to them from somewhere beyond the door, then footsteps hurrying closer.

That finally made Ghalander realize the urgency of their situation. He ran for the window and started to clamber through it.

Dastan heard the door fly open and realized they were in trouble. Ghalander was still struggling to climb out; there was no way Dastan would have time to follow. Not without shoving the other boy out and sending him plummeting to his certain death, anyway.

He lunged toward the table, grabbing the pair of dinner knives he'd seen there. Clutching one in each hand, he backed away from the door as Babak and Murdad burst in.

"You!" Murdad roared.

"Get him!" Babak added, leaping forward.

Dastan was ready for him, whipping the knives back and forth as he dodged to one side. Babak let out a yelp and jumped back.

"He's got weapons!" Babak cried.

"It's still two against one," Murdad growled. "And he's just a boy!"

Glancing over, Dastan realized the taller man was sidling around him. Acting fast, he slashed at Babak again. Babak dodged to avoid the flying blades, and Dastan dashed for the door.

"Get back here, street rat!" Babak howled.

Dastan barely saw the next room as he raced through it. He was totally focused on the window on the far side. Sprinting toward it, he dove through without bothering to check what was on the other side.

He hung in the air for a moment, just long

enough to glance down and spy a low rooftop. Pumping his legs, he somersaulted down and landed on his feet. He hit hard and skidded down the steep slope. Just as he was about to fly off into the alley below, he shoved the points of the knives he was still holding into the roof and then pushed off as hard as he could, flinging himself onto the roof across the way. He caught himself again with the knives and jumped to his feet.

Behind him, he could hear Babak and Murdad yelling. He didn't look back, racing across roof after roof until the angry voices faded away.

When he finally stopped to catch his breath, he realized he was almost at the eastern wall. It rose steeply just beyond the next building.

He tucked the knives into his belt and peered up. While the outside of the wall was polished smooth to help repel intruders, Dastan saw that the inside had been less carefully constructed. In this particular spot, there were plenty of rough areas, perhaps enough to offer a handhold. . . .

Soon Dastan was crawling up the wall like a human spider. A few times he almost slipped or lost his grip. But his years of experience scrambling up and down the walls of Nasaf paid off, and he made it to the top.

He stuck his head out to look for guards. The only one in view was standing on the narrow walkway atop the wall some fifty yards away, his back to Dastan.

Dastan slithered silently up onto the wall's rim and stood staring out at the beckoning freedom of the moonlit landscape below. His mind raced with all that had just happened. Finding Vindarna's name in his enemies' papers had been a shock, especially after the way the Magian had insisted that he'd never heard of

Kazem. Could Vindarna be plotting against him now because of another such prophecy? Dastan had no idea, but it seemed more important than ever to get out of Babylon by any means necessary.

He glanced down and saw the impossibly high, smooth wall stretching down toward the ground. It was made to keep enemies out, and all possible handholds had been sanded away.

"Hey! Guards!" a voice shouted out from behind and below him.

Spinning around, he saw Babak and Murdad clambering over the rooftops. Babak was waving at the nearest guards atop the wall, shouting for their attention.

Dastan glanced to the left. The guard he'd spotted before was already turning to peer at him. To the right, two more guards had just hurried into view along the rampart. Looking below him, Dastan saw that Murdad was already climbing up the inside wall, while Babak was jumping up and down and shaking his fist.

"Give up, boy!" Babak's voice crowed. "You're trapped!"

He was right. The guards were running toward him now from both directions; they would be on him in seconds. If he tried to escape back down the inside of the wall, Murdad and Babak would intercept him.

There was no way out.

Or was there? With all the guards up on the wall, perhaps he'd have a head start. He made his decision.

"Good-bye, Babylon!" Dastan cried out.

Then he crouched and pushed off, leaping into the air.

CHAPTER TEN

"Aaaaaaah!" Dastan cried as he plummeted downward.

Scrabbling around at his waist, he managed to pull out the knives he'd tucked in his belt. He twisted his body around in midair....

WHAM!

The points of both knives dug into the wall. They scraped and sparked, and for a second Dastan thought this wasn't going to work.

But he flung his weight toward the wall, and finally the sturdy blades dug in deeply enough to stop his fall. He hung there for a second, panting with fear and adrenaline.

Then he carefully unwedged one of the knives.

THUNK! He plunged it into the wall again a little lower. Then he repeated the process with the other knife. In this way he started inching himself slowly, carefully, down the sheer wall.

"Stop!" Someone shouted from above. "In the name of the ancient laws of Babylon!"

Glancing up, Dastan saw a guard peering down at him. "Sorry," he called to him. "I've got to be going."

Two or three more guards appeared beside the first. Then Murdad joined them.

"Get back here, boy!" he called in a hoarse, angry shout.

Dastan ignored him. A second later, something pinged off the wall a few feet from his head. With no other way to reach him, Murdad was now throwing stones at him.

Dastan almost laughed out loud. A few rocks wouldn't hurt him. He was going to make it! And then . . .

"Bring the boiling oil!" Murdad shouted to the guards.

Dastan glanced down. He still had a long way to go, and it sounded as if he'd better pick up the pace.

Thunk, thunk. He yanked the knives out and stuck them back in as quickly as he could. One of Murdad's stones hit him on the shoulder, but he ignored the sting. Above, he could hear the thud of running feet.

"Oil's here!" a guard shouted. "Help us get it in position!"

Dastan gulped. He was still some seventy feet above the ground, and he was running out of time.

Taking a deep breath, he braced himself— and then let go of both knives. He did his best to press himself against the wall as he skidded down it, faster and faster. Finally, when he judged that the moment was right, he pushed off hard with both feet. Tucking his body into a ball, he somersaulted backward through the air, over and over. . . .

He hit the ground hard with both feet, overbalancing and falling forward onto his face.

SZZZZZZ!

The first droplets of boiling oil splattered down around him. Dastan let out a yelp as one landed on his shoulder, burning him through his clothes. Springing up like a desert hare, he did several handsprings in a row away from the wall.

And just in time. The bulk of the oil poured down right where he'd landed, burning a hole in the hard-packed dirt and sending up a cloud of acrid smoke.

But without a backward glance, Dastan was

already running into the darkness. He wasn't sure where he was going, but he was relieved to be free of Babylon—he hoped forever.

The scorching sun burned high over the desert when Dastan finally spotted the oasis on the horizon. He staggered forward, willing himself to reach it before he collapsed from thirst and exhaustion. He'd spent the last several days on the move, afraid to stop until he'd left the fertile fields of Babylon behind and once more reached the familiar heat and sand of the desert.

"Look!" someone called out as he neared the line of palms marking the boundary of the oasis. "Someone's approaching on foot, all alone!"

Dastan blinked, trying to force his sun-weary eyes to focus as two or three people rushed toward him. He knew he had to stay alert; what if they were enemies?

But it was no use. As the first set of hands grabbed for him, he slipped away into blissful darkness.

"Hello," a kind female voice said when Dastan opened his eyes some time later.

He blinked and sat up quickly. A pretty young woman was sitting in the sand beside him. She was holding a water jug.

"Who are you?" Dastan blurted out. "Where am I?"

"He's awake!" the woman called over her shoulder. Then she smiled and held the water out to Dastan. "Here, drink."

Grabbing the jug, he tipped it upward, allowing the cool, delicious water to pour down his parched throat. As he drank, he glanced around and saw that they were in the heart of the oasis. He'd been lying in the shade of a shrubby palm near a spring. A dozen people were bustling around, while several camels dozed and chewed their cuds nearby.

"My name is Laleh," the woman said when he'd quenched his thirst. "You're lucky we saw you coming. What were you doing out in the desert all alone?"

Dastan didn't answer, wiping droplets of water from his lips. *All alone.* That described him perfectly, didn't it? He thought briefly of Javed, his one true friend, gone forever. Then he thought of Ghalander, the new friend he'd left behind. He hoped Ghalander had escaped through that window without being seen by Babak and Murdad, but he supposed he would never know for sure. It made him sad to realize that the two of them would almost certainly never cross paths again. Another friend lost forever . . .

"Where did you come from?" Dastan asked the woman warily, forcing his mind back to the here and now. "Are you from Babylon?"

"No," Laleh replied. "My husband and I hail originally from Izadkhast, though most of the others come from a small farming community southwest of here. Our destination is Bishapur."

Bishapur. Dastan felt a jolt as he realized that was the nearest city to Cyra's family farm.

He also remembered something else—that parchment he'd retrieved from Babak and Murdad. He reached into his clothes, checking that it was still there.

It was, but that didn't make him feel much better. He still wasn't sure what Babak and Murdad were up to, with their connection to Kazem, their mysterious plots and prophecies, and their desire to smear his name. But one thing he did know. If the men remembered the address written on this parchment and connected Cyra to Dastan, they might decide to search for him there. That meant Cyra and her whole family were in danger—all because of him.

He knew what he had to do.

"I have business near Bishapur myself," he told Laleh. "Will you take me with you?"

Dastan's journey, it would seem, had only just begun.

Dastan's adventure is destined to continue.

Join the excitement in. . . .

THE SEARCH for CYRA

By Catherine Hapka
Based on characters created for the motion picture
Prince of Persia: The Sands of Time
Based on the Screenplay written by Boaz Yakin and Doug Miro & Carlo Bernard
Screen Story by Jordan Mechner
Based on the videogame series "Prince Of Persia" created by Jordan Mechner
Executive Producers Mike Stenson, Chad Oman, John August,
Jordan Mechner, Patrick McCormick, Eric McLeod
Produced by Jerry Bruckheimer
Directed by Mike Newell

Turn the page to get a sneak peek. . . .

CHAPTER ONE

Dastan leaned on the sill of the palace window and enjoyed the cool evening breeze. Nasaf lay before him, its rooftops bathed in the coppery glow of the sun setting behind the city's high western wall.

"More dates, Dastan?"

He glanced over his shoulder. His friend Cyra had just hurried in, carrying two platters piled high with food. She set them on the table, which was already groaning under the weight of delicacies of every description—fragrant pomegranates, juicy and succulent kebabs, bowls of steaming rice sprinkled with fresh herbs. The food was piled so high that Dastan could hardly see the luxurious woven rugs hanging on the far wall of the well-appointed sitting room.

"Thanks," Dastan said, stifling a burp. "Where's Ghalander?"

Cyra rolled her eyes as she set down the platters and pushed a strand of dark hair out of her face. "You know him," she said. "He's curious about everything! Now he's asking the palace astronomers whether they can predict the coming of the next solar eclipse."

Dastan chuckled. That indeed sounded like Ghalander. In fact, the other boy's curiosity had led to their friendship—and Dastan's escape from Babylon!*

His smile faded. Why did the thought of the distant city trigger such a feeling of dread

*This escape occurred in Volume 1, *Walls of Babylon*.

in the pit of his stomach? Before he could figure it out, a servant entered the room.

"Begging your pardon, sir," the servant said, bowing to Dastan. "Prince Tus and Prince Garsiv are taking an evening stroll through the gardens and would be honored if you would join them."

"Thank you. Since I'm finished, I'll go out and find them now." Dastan glanced at Cyra. "Want to come?"

"I'll join you in a few minutes," she said. "I'm still hungry."

Dastan nodded. Grabbing a handful of dates—after all, he never knew when he'd be hungry again—he popped them into his pocket and headed out. He passed through the palace's maze of rooms and staircases as quickly and easily as he'd once navigated the dusty roof-tops of Nasaf, and he soon emerged into the palaces expansive walled gardens.

Ahhh ... He couldn't resist stopping to take in the strong scents of the exotic flowering plants King Sharaman had brought in from all over the Persian Empire and beyond. The air was rich with the chirping of insects and the musical calls of unseen birds.

It was all so beautiful it almost seemed unreal. A feeling of peace washed over Dastan as he realized he now had everything he'd ever wished for or dreamed of back when he'd had to struggle merely to survive on the streets. . . .

Then came a soft footstep behind him. Dastan turned, expecting to see the princes, or perhaps Ghalander or Cyra.

Instead, he was just in time to notice the sharp edge of a curved sword swinging toward him! Honed by years on the street, his reflexes kicked in, and he ducked just in time. The metal blade swished right over his head!

"Kazem!" Dastan blurted out as he saw who

wielded the sword—a man who was dressed in the rich robes of Persia's upper classes and had a malicious sneer on his lips.*

"Stand still, boy," Kazem growled. "Can't you see I'm trying to kill you?"

Dastan felt fear and anger rush through him. The man seemed determined to see him dead at any cost!

"You thought you could escape your fate so easily?" Kazem snapped. "You fool."

A chuckle came out of the darkness, and Dastan turned just in time to dodge a dagger as it flew at him. Kazem's cohort Babak stepped into view a second later.

"Young Dastan *is* a silly thing, isn't he?" Babak chortled, clutching his rotund belly with glee. "Still, what do you expect from a lowly Nasaf street rat? He can't even die properly!"

---

* Kazem was the mysterious man who sent Dastan on a dangerous fool's errand to Babylon in Volume 1.

Dastan glanced over his shoulder and saw a third man—Babak's partner, Murdad—swing a rough wooden club toward his head. Beneath heavy brows, Murdad's eyes glittered with malice. Dastan was surrounded! "No!" he cried, somersaulting out of the way.

CRASH! The club smashed down on a decorative birdbath, narrowly missing Dastan and sending shards of stone flying.

Dastan's head was spinning. What were Babak and Murdad doing here in Nasaf? The last time he'd seen them they were in Babylon... halfway across the empire!